Jenny McLachlan

Illustrated by **Gustavo Mazali**

UNIVERSITY PRESS

A long time ago, my husband and I stayed at an elephant sanctuary in Thailand. We peeled corn on the cob for the elephants and scrubbed them down in the river. Our dog was called Belly, and I loved her even though she had a lot of fleas (it's better to have fleas in your room than snakes!).

They were happy, magical days, and so different to our lives in England as teachers. One day, an elephant called Boy got annoyed with the dogs who were darting around his feet ... what happened next inspired the story you're about to read.

Jenny McLachlan

Chapter One

It was the last day of school before the summer holidays. Charkris was on the field with the other boys in the Year Four class. They were all there except Jonah. He was drifting around on his own as usual.

The sun was beating down and no one could decide what to do.

Suddenly, Oliver said, 'Look at Jonah.'

Jonah was smiling as he studied something he'd found in the grass. Charkris was about to suggest that they go and see what he had spotted, when Oliver started laughing.

'Jonah's so weird!' he said, then he began telling them all about his holiday. 'We're going to Spain for two weeks,' he boasted, 'and we're staying in a *massive* hotel. It's got three pools!'

'I'm going camping,' said Will.

But Oliver carried on talking as if Will hadn't spoken. 'At the hotel you can have anything you want to eat or drink. Anything at all!'

The other boys nodded. They were impressed.

'Shall we play tag before our last lesson?' asked Will.

'Too hot,' said Oliver, and that was that. Oliver always decided what they did.

Then everyone fell quiet, even Oliver, so Charkris said, 'I'm going to Thailand this summer. I'm staying with my nan. She runs an elephant rescue centre and I'm going to help look after them.'

'Really?' said Will. 'I'd love to do that!'

Suddenly Oliver jumped to his feet. 'Bet your nan hasn't got three swimming pools,' he said. 'Come on, let's play tag. I'm "it".'

Charkris followed Oliver and the others into the middle of the field. Oliver was right, he thought. There weren't any swimming pools at his nan's place, but there was a wide brown river that he liked to float down in a rubber ring.

Often the elephants were in the river too and Charkris got sprayed by the water they blew out of their trunks. He'd love to tell Oliver and the other boys about this, but there was no point. They never listened to him.

Chapter Two

By the time Charkris and his mum had been in Thailand for two weeks, school seemed like a million miles away.

Charkris was helping the other volunteers peel corn for the elephants to eat. A warm breeze blew over them. They were in a hut with open sides. It was raised off the ground in case the river flooded. The hut was surrounded by mountains and the sound of chattering insects.

Charkris reached for another corn cob and peeled away its stringy covering. He did it as quickly as he could because the elephants were getting hungry. The large grey creatures circled the hut. Sometimes they rested their chins on the hut floor. Sometimes their trunks would snake towards the corn, even though they weren't allowed to eat yet.

Charkris felt something soft brush past his ankle. A young elephant called Boy was tickling his foot with his trunk. Warm air rushed over Charkris's bare toes. 'Nearly ready,' he laughed, reaching forwards to scratch the elephant's huge, rough head.

Boy's beady eyes glittered and his trunk twisted around Charkris's arm. Most of the elephants at the sanctuary had been rescued from places where tourists could pay for elephant rides, but Boy was different. He had been born at the sanctuary and he and Charkris were old friends.

'Looks like Boy wants some attention,' said Charkris's nan, crouching down next to him. She wore baggy trousers and a cotton T-shirt. Her skin was brown and as wrinkled as Boy's. 'Sorry there aren't any other kids for you to play with, Charkris. I hope you don't get lonely here.'

Charkris looked around him. The volunteers were laughing at a joke someone had made, and his mum was reading a book. To his surprise, Charkris realized that he felt lonelier at school than he did here, even though he hardly knew the other volunteers.

But he didn't tell Nan this. He didn't want her to worry. Instead he said, 'I'm not lonely. I've got all the dogs to play with.'

Nan laughed. 'There are *a lot* of dogs here!'

Stray dogs kept arriving at the rescue centre and Charkris's nan couldn't turn them away. There were at least thirty-five. The dogs stuck close to the volunteers who fed them treats. They slept in the volunteers' rooms at night and helped keep the rats and snakes away.

'Where's Belly?' asked Nan. Belly was Charkris's favourite dog. She was small and white with ginger spots on her big tummy.

Charkris gestured to the riverbank where Belly was playing on her own. She chased a bird then flopped down in the mud and closed her eyes.

'Belly doesn't stick with the pack,' Nan said.

'Why not?' asked Charkris. 'Are they mean to her?'

Nan laughed. 'No, she's just happier away from the others. They're a noisy bunch.'

Charkris thought about the chaotic games of football and tag that happened at school. He always played them even though he didn't enjoy them much. Then he thought about Jonah. He was usually on his own, but he looked happy. Perhaps Jonah was like Belly and didn't like being part of a pack.

All of a sudden, the dogs started to growl and snap at each other.

'Feeding time!' said Nan. Then she reached out a hand to Charkris. 'Coming to help?'

Chapter Three

The rest of the holiday was even better than Charkris had expected. Dad arrived and they took the elephants up into the mountains. They camped in a hut and stayed up late, listening to the elephants moving around in the darkness. Back at the sanctuary, Charkris helped Nan with the elephants while his parents relaxed. They were happy days. They were exciting days. A snake even fell on Mum's head while she was having a shower!

But all too soon, Charkris was saying goodbye to Nan at the airport.

'Boy and Belly will be waiting for you next year,' Nan said, squeezing him tight. 'Call me!'

Charkris had a few quiet days back in England before he returned to school. When the first day of term arrived, it was strange putting on his stiff school shoes after so many days of running around barefoot.

At lunchtime, Charkris and the boys in his class went to their usual corner of the field. Oliver told them about a zoo he had visited on holiday in Spain. 'We bought popcorn and fed it to the animals. A goat chased me for more!'

Charkris looked up. He was only half-listening – Oliver's stories went on for a long time. He suddenly thought of something he could tell everyone.

'I got chased by an elephant in Thailand,' he blurted out.

'What?' They all turned to look at him.

'It happened when I fed the dogs,' he said. 'About thirty of the dogs were following me to the hut where we kept their food—'

'Hang on,' said Will, interrupting him. Then he called out to the other kids playing near them, 'Come and listen to this: Charkris got chased by an elephant!'

More children wandered over. Jonah came too, and stood at the edge of the group.

Charkris took a deep breath and carried on. 'So I was walking towards this hut with all these dogs around me, when I felt the ground shake.'

Then Charkris forgot about the staring faces, and he was back in Thailand. The sun was beating down, dogs were jostling against his legs and the ground was thudding beneath his bare feet.

'I turned and saw an elephant charging towards me. It was Boy. He's a young elephant so he's not massive, but he's strong. His ears were stretched out and his trunk was raised so I knew he wasn't happy.' Charkris remembered how scared he was when he saw Boy racing towards him.

'What did you do?' Kanda, a girl in his class, asked excitedly.

'I ran!' he said, and everyone laughed. 'I ran towards the hut, but the dogs followed me. The hut was on stilts and as I climbed the wooden ladder, the dogs came too. They nearly knocked me off it.' Charkris remembered panicking as he fought his way past the dogs to get to safety.

'Then what?' said Kanda.

'Boy started bashing the posts holding up the hut and it rocked from side to side. I thought the hut was going to collapse!'

'But it didn't?' said Will.

Charkris shook his head. 'My nan came and whispered in Boy's ear. She's looked after elephants all her life. She knows how to calm them down.'

'That is so cool,' said Kanda, her eyes wide. The other children nodded in agreement.

Then Oliver announced, 'Charkris is lying. He never got chased by an elephant. He's making it up.'

Charkris felt sick. His heart thudded and
his cheeks grew hot as the other children
stared at him. 'I'm not,' he managed to say.

'Why would elephants be wandering
around?' said Oliver. 'They're dangerous.
They would be in cages like the one I saw at
the zoo in Spain.'

'They're not dangerous,' protested Charkris. 'They've never chased me before. Boy was annoyed by the dogs. They wouldn't stop barking and—'

'All thirty of them?' said Oliver, one eyebrow raised. 'Are you sure there weren't a hundred?' The group who had gathered around shifted uneasily. Someone laughed. 'Come on,' said Oliver. 'Let's play tag.'

Obediently, most of the other boys and a few of the girls followed Oliver across the field.

'Are you going to play?' Will asked Charkris.

Charkris looked at Oliver walking at the front of the pack of children.

He shook his head. 'No. I don't feel like it.'

'Neither do I,' said Will, and he sat down.

Just then, they heard a voice. It was Jonah.

'Charkris,' he said. 'What does an elephant's skin feel like?'

Charkris took one last look at Oliver, who was organizing the game, and then he turned to Jonah and smiled. 'It feels like the bark of a tree, only it's softer and hot from the sun.'

Jonah grinned, then Will said, 'What about their trunks? Do they really spray water out of them?'

They talked all lunchtime. Will chatted about his trip to Scotland and Jonah told them about his pet snake. (It went missing during the holidays then turned up in one of his rollerblades.)

When the bell rang, they walked together into their classroom. The game of tag was breaking up, but Charkris and the others hardly noticed. They were too busy talking about a game they were going to play tomorrow – Snakes and Elephants.

Charkris couldn't wait.